D1450255

HALIFAX COUNTY · SOUTH BOSTON
REGIONAL LIBRARY
HALIFAX, VIRGINIA

J
791.45
C

CAVERNS OF FEAR

by MARY CAREY

illustrated by AL McWILLIAMS

GOLDEN PRESS · NEW YORK
Western Publishing Company, Inc., Racine, Wisconsin

Copyright © Mattel, Inc. 1983. All Rights Reserved. MASTERS OF THE UNIVERSE, HE-MAN, BATTLE CAT, CASTLE GRAYSKULL, MER-MAN, SKELETOR, TEELA, BEAST MAN, TRAP JAW, MAN-AT-ARMS, and STRATOS are trademarks owned by and used under license from Mattel, Inc. Printed in the U.S.A. by Western Publishing Company, Inc. No part of this book may be reproduced or copied in any form without written permission from the publisher. Golden,® and Golden Press® are trademarks of Western Publishing Company, Inc. Library of Congress Catalog Card Number 83-80915. ISBN 0-307-11794-4/ISBN 0-307-61974-5 (lib. bdg.) B C D E F G H I J

134188
E.4

The great Castle Grayskull loomed on the horizon — seeming to grin. Locked within the fortress since the time of the Elders were the mystical secrets of ages past. Legend foretold that whoever controlled Grayskull's halls would gain mastery over all the forces of the universe.

As dawn broke, He-Man — powerful foe of the forces of evil
— raced across the plains of Eternia astride the mighty
Battle Cat. For the moment at least, the strife-torn planet
seemed almost peaceful. So He-Man seized the time
to give the fighting tiger a vigorous workout.

"What's this?" cried He-Man. "Why are you stopping?"
He-Man spied a well then, not far from the castle wall.
"Battle Cat wants a drink, does he?" said He-Man.
"Just like any spoiled kitten! Perhaps I will trade you for
a Wind Raider!"

Battle Cat growled a pitiful growl.

"Oh, very well," laughed He-Man, and he drew up a
bucket of water.

As Battle Cat drank, strange sounds emerged from the well.

At the bottom of the well, He-Man found
rushing stream. Beyond the stream was
passage, low and dark.

"Caverns!" exclaimed He-Man. "Once I heard it whispered th
there were caves under Castle Grayskull — caves so deep that
man might be lost in them forever. The tale is true!"

He-Man started toward the tunnel.

Suddenly a monstrous shape rose from the water behind him!

It was Mer-Man, the dreaded Sea-Lord. He tried to drag He-Man under the surface of the stream.

"Back, you monster!" shouted He-Man, knowing even as he spoke that the evil Skeletor could not be far away.

But the foul sea demon clung fast.

He-Man was too close to swing his Power Sword, but he managed to free one arm...

...which he brought down on Mer-Man's head!

THAK

Mer-Man fell into the stream, stunned. The current caught him and carried him away.

He-Man raced into the black and beckoning passageway. Somewhere in the caverns ahead, there was a battle going on!

Moments later He-Man found himself entering a huge underground chamber.

In that chamber, He-Man saw his arch enemy Skeletor, Lord of Destruction. He was battling the warrior-maiden Teela, who had seen him steal into the well and followed him into the caverns.

"He-Man! Thank heaven you're here!" Teela cried. "Skeletor plans to enter Castle Grayskull through this cavern!"

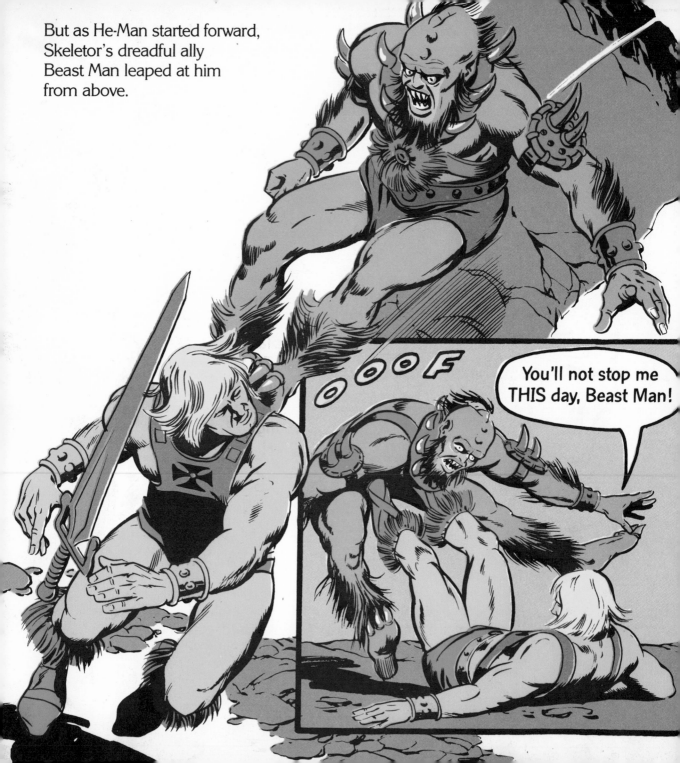

Beast Man reeled backward toward a deep pit in the floor of the cave. He teetered there for a moment, and then fell!

AAAYIII

He-Man snatched his sword from the dust where it had fallen, and found himself face to face with Skeletor!

Once again you interfere with my plans, He-Man. This time I will put an END to your meddling... forever!

The very ground shook
as the swords of power
clashed in battle.

While He-Man and
Skeletor faced
off in their struggle,
Trap Jaw, Skeletor's
henchman, took Teela
by surprise!

But the warrior-maiden was well trained, and Skeletor's servant found that he had a fight on his hands.

Soon, however, Trap Jaw regained the advantage. He seized Teela, and swung around to face He-Man.

"Yield, He-Man!" he threatened, as his steel arm tightened around her body.

Release her!" boomed a voice from the mouth of the tunnel. Trap Jaw turned to find Man-at-Arms approaching — swinging his mace!

An instant later Stratos, the winged warrior, soared into the cavern.

With split-second timing he lifted Teela out of harm's way.

He-Man returned to the fight. He charged at Skeletor. As he swung the Power Sword, however, the fiendish Lord of Destruction vanished. A green mist hung where he had stood. There seemed no end to his magic powers.

"We are safe for now my friends," said He-Man. "Thanks to you, Skeletor has fled. He has no stomach for *even* fights! Still, we must make sure no one ever tries to enter Castle Grayskull this way again."

He-Man's sword flashed out. Again and again he struck at the stone formations in the cavern.

R-RUMBLE

There was a rumbling from above. The earth trembled as the walls began to cave in!

The Masters of the Universe fled down the dark passageway to the well. Behind them the caverns echoed and boomed as they filled with rocks and dirt. The underground passage to Castle Grayskull was gone now, sealed forever.

Battle Cat was waiting at the top of the well. "You are a faithful animal," said He-Man, "waiting patiently all this time."

"A *clever* animal, you mean," said Man-at-Arms. "It was *he* who found us in the forest. When we saw him alone we were afraid for you. He led us here."

"So!" said He-Man, "a live cat *is* a better steed than a machine. He *may* need water, but there is much he can do that a machine cannot!"

At this, Battle Cat gave a great, rumbling purr. Then the warriors parted.

HALIFAX COUNTY · SOUTH BOST
REGIONAL LIBRARY
HALIFAX, VIRGINIA

"We've not seen the last of Skeletor!" said He-Man, knowing the Lord of Destruction would strike again.

"We'll be ready for him," replied Teela, as a strange quiet fell over the plains of Eternia.